RAINBOW magic

RAINBOW FAIRIES 1-4

RUBY
the Red Fairy

AMBER
the Orange Fairy

SUNNY
the Yellow Fairy

FERN
the Green Fairy

By Daisy Meadows

Illustrated by Georgie Ripper

Silver Dolphin

Silver Dolphin Books
An imprint of Printers Row Publishing Group
A division of Readerlink Distribution Services, LLC
9717 Pacific Heights Blvd, San Diego, CA 92121
www.silverdolphinbooks.com

Printers Row Publishing Group is a division of
Readerlink Distribution Services, LLC.
Silver Dolphin Books is a registered trademark of
Readerlink Distribution Services, LLC.

All notations of errors or omissions should be addressed to Silver
Dolphin Books, Editorial Department, at the above address. All other
correspondence (author inquiries, permissions) concerning the
content of this book should be addressed to:
Hachette Children's Group
Carmelite House
50 Victoria Embankment
London
EC4Y 0DZ

ISBN: 978-1-6672-0143-6
Manufactured, printed, and assembled in Heshan, China.
First printing, February 2022. LP/02/22
26 25 24 23 22 1 2 3 4 5

Table of Contents

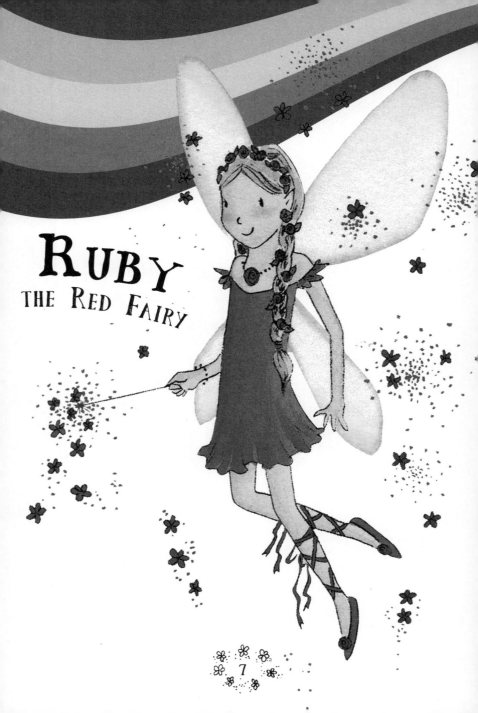

RUBY
THE RED FAIRY

Cold winds blow and thick ice form,
I conjure up this fairy storm.
To seven corners of the human world
the Rainbow Fairies will be hurled!

I curse every part of Fairyland,
with a frosty wave of my icy hand.
For now and always, from this day,
Fairyland will be cold and gray!

Table of Contents

THE END OF THE RAINBOW

"Look, Dad!" said Rachel Walker. She
pointed across the blue-green sea at the
rocky island ahead of them. The ferry was
sailing toward it, dipping up and down
on the rolling waves. "Is that Rainspell
Island?" she asked.

Her dad nodded. "Yes, it is," he said,
smiling. "Our vacation is about to begin!"

The waves slapped against the side
of the ferry as it bobbed up and down on
the water. Rachel felt her heart thump with
excitement. She could see white cliffs and
emerald-green fields on the island. And
golden sandy beaches, with tide pools here
and there.

Suddenly, a few raindrops plopped down
on Rachel's head. "Oh!" she gasped,
surprised. The sun was still shining.

Rachel's mom grabbed her hand. "Let's get under cover," she said, leading Rachel inside.

"Isn't that strange?" Rachel said. "Sunshine *and* rain!"

"Let's hope the rain stops before we get off the ferry," said Mr. Walker. "Now, where did I put that map of the island?"

Rachel looked out of the window. Her eyes opened wide.

A girl was standing alone on the deck. Her dark hair was wet with raindrops, but she didn't seem to care. She just stared up at the sky.

Rachel looked over at her mom
and dad. They were busy studying
the map. So Rachel slipped back
outside to see what was so interesting.

And there it was.

In the blue sky, high above them,
was the most amazing rainbow that
Rachel had ever seen. One end of
the rainbow stretched far out to sea.
The other seemed to fall somewhere
on Rainspell Island. All of the colors
were bright and clear.

THE END OF THE RAINBOW

Red
Orange
Yellow
Green
Blue
Indigo
Violet

"Isn't it perfect?" the dark-haired girl whispered to Rachel.

"Yes, it is," Rachel agreed. "Are you going to Rainspell on vacation?"

The girl nodded. "We're staying for a week," she said. "I'm Kirsty Tate."

Rachel smiled as the rain began to stop. "I'm Rachel Walker. We're staying at Mermaid Cottage," she added.

"Oh! We're at Dolphin Cottage," said Kirsty. "Do you think we might be close to each other?"

"I hope so," Rachel replied. She had a feeling she was going to like Kirsty.

Kirsty leaned over the rail and looked down into the shimmering water. "The ocean looks really deep here, doesn't it?" she said. "There might even be mermaids down there, watching us right now!"

Rachel stared at the waves. She saw
something that made her heart skip a beat.
"Look!" she said. "Is that a mermaid's
hair?" Then she laughed when she saw
that it was just seaweed.

"It could be a mermaid's necklace," said
Kirsty, smiling. "Maybe she lost
it when she was trying to escape from
a sea monster."

The ferry was now sailing
into Rainspell's tiny
harbor. Seagulls flew
around them, and
fishing boats bobbed
on the water.
"Look at that
big white cliff over
there," Kirsty said.
She pointed it out
to Rachel.
"It looks like
a giant's face,
doesn't it?"
Rachel
looked, and
nodded. Kirsty
seemed to see
magic *everywhere*.

"There you are, Rachel!" called Mrs. Walker. Rachel turned around and saw her mom and dad coming out onto the deck. "We'll be getting off the ferry in a few minutes," Mrs. Walker added.

"Mom, Dad, this is Kirsty," Rachel said. "She's staying at Dolphin Cottage."

"That's right next door to ours," said Mr. Walker. "I remember seeing it on the map."

Rachel and Kirsty looked at each other and smiled.

"I'd better go and find *my* mom and dad," said Kirsty. She looked around. "Oh, there they are."

Kirsty's mom and dad came over to say hello to the Walkers. Then the ferry docked, and everyone began to leave the boat.

"Our cottages are on the other side of the harbor," said Rachel's dad, looking at the map. "It's not too far."

Mermaid Cottage and Dolphin Cottage were right next to the beach. Rachel loved her bedroom, which was high up in the attic. From the window, she could see the waves rolling onto the sand.

A shout from outside made Rachel look down. It was Kirsty. She was standing under the window, waving.

"Let's go and explore the beach!" Kirsty called.

Rachel dashed outside to join her.

Piles of seaweed lay on the sand, and there were tiny pink-and-white shells sprinkled everywhere.

"I love it here already!" Rachel shouted happily above the noise of the seagulls.

"Me too," Kirsty said. She pointed up at the sky. "Look, the rainbow's still there."

Rachel looked up. The rainbow glowed brightly among the fluffy white clouds.

"Have you heard the story about the pot of gold at the end of the rainbow?" Kirsty asked.

Rachel nodded. "Yes, but that's just in fairy tales," she said.

Kirsty grinned. "Maybe. But let's go and find out for ourselves!"

"OK," Rachel agreed. "And maybe we can explore the island at the same time."

They rushed back to tell their parents
where they were going. Then Kirsty
and Rachel set off along a road behind
the cottages. It led them away from the
beach, across green fields, and toward a
small stretch of woods.

Rachel kept looking up at the rainbow. She was worried that it would start to fade now that the rain had stopped. But the colors stayed clear and bright.

"It looks like the end of the rainbow is over there," Kirsty said. "Come on!" And she hurried toward the trees.

The woods were cool and shady after being in the heat of the sun. Rachel and Kirsty followed a winding path until they came to a clearing. Then they both stopped and stared.

The rainbow shone down onto the grass through a gap in the trees. Its colors sparkled and twinkled brightly.

And there, at the rainbow's end, lay an old, black pot.

A TINY SURPRISE

"Look!" Kirsty whispered. "There really *is* a pot of gold!"

"It could just be a cooking pot," Rachel said doubtfully. "Some campers might have left it behind."

But Kirsty shook her head. "I don't think so," she said. "It looks really old."

Rachel stared at the pot. It was sitting on the grass, upside down.

"Let's have a closer look," said Kirsty. She ran to the pot and tried to turn it over. "Oh, it's heavy!" she gasped. She tried again, but the pot didn't move.

Rachel rushed to help her. They both pushed and pushed at the pot. This time it moved, but just a little.

"Let's try again," Kirsty panted. "Are you ready, Rachel?"

Tap! Tap! Tap!

Rachel and Kirsty stared at each other.

"What was that?" Rachel gasped.

"I don't know," whispered Kirsty.

Tap! Tap!

"There it is again," Kirsty said. She looked down at the pot lying on the grass. "You know what? I think it's coming from inside this pot!"

Rachel's eyes opened wide. "Are you sure?" She bent down, and put her ear to the pot. *Tap! Tap!* Then, to her amazement, Rachel heard a tiny voice.

"Help!" it called. "Help me!"

Rachel grabbed Kirsty's arm. "Did you hear that?" she asked.

Kirsty nodded. "Quick!" she said. "We have to turn the pot over, somehow!"

Rachel and Kirsty pushed at the pot as hard as they could. It began to rock from side to side on the grass.

"We're almost there!" Rachel cried. "Keep pushing, Kirsty!"

The girls pushed with all their might. Suddenly, the pot turned over and rolled onto its side. Rachel and Kirsty were taken by surprise. They both lost their balance and landed on the grass with a thump.

"Look!" Kirsty whispered, breathing hard.

A small shower of sparkling red dust had flown out of the pot. Rachel and Kirsty gasped with surprise. The dust hung in the air above them. And there, right in the middle of the glittering cloud, was a tiny, winged girl.

Rachel and Kirsty watched in wonder as the tiny girl fluttered in the sunlight. Her delicate wings sparkled with all the colors of the rainbow.

"Oh, Rachel!" Kirsty whispered. "It's a fairy . . ."

FAIRY MAGIC

The fairy flew over Rachel and Kirsty's heads. Her short, silky dress was the color of ripe strawberries. Red crystal earrings glowed in her ears. Her golden hair was braided with tiny red roses, and she wore crimson slippers on her little feet.

The fairy waved her scarlet wand, and a shower of sparkling red fairy dust floated softly down to the ground. Where the dust landed, all kinds of red flowers appeared with a *pop*!

Rachel and Kirsty watched open mouthed. This really and truly *was* a fairy.

"This is like a dream," Rachel said.

"I always believed in fairies," Kirsty whispered back. "But I never thought I'd ever *see* one!"

The fairy flew toward them. "Oh, thank you *so* much!" she called in a tiny voice. "I'm free at last!" She glided down and landed on Kirsty's hand.

Kirsty gasped. The fairy felt lighter and softer than a butterfly.

"I was beginning to think I'd *never* get out of the pot!" the fairy said.

Kirsty wanted to ask the fairy so many things. But she didn't know where to start.

"Tell me your names, quickly," said the fairy. She fluttered up into the air again. "There's so much to be done, and we must get started right away."

Rachel wondered what the fairy meant. "I'm Rachel," she said.

"And I'm Kirsty," said Kirsty. "But who are *you*?"

"I'm the Red Rainbow Fairy—but you can call me Ruby," the fairy replied.

"Ruby. . . " Kirsty breathed. "A Rainbow Fairy. . . " She and Rachel stared at each other in excitement. This really *was* magic!

"Yes," said Ruby. "And I have six sisters: Amber, Sunny, Fern, Sky, Inky, and Heather. One for each color of the rainbow, you see."

"What do Rainbow Fairies do?" Rachel asked.

Ruby flew over and landed lightly on Rachel's hand. "It's our job to put all the different colors into Fairyland," she explained.

"So why were you trapped under that old pot?" asked Rachel.

"And where are your sisters?" Kirsty added.

Ruby's golden wings drooped. Her eyes filled with tiny, sparkling tears. "I don't know," she said. "Something terrible has happened in Fairyland. We *really* need your help!"

FAIRIES IN DANGER

Kirsty stared down at Ruby, sitting sadly on Rachel's hand. "Of course we'll help you!" she said.

"Just tell us how," added Rachel.

Ruby wiped the tears from her eyes. "Thank you!" she said. "But first I must show you the terrible thing that has happened. Follow me—as quickly as you can!" She flew into the air, her wings shimmering in the sunshine.

Rachel and Kirsty followed Ruby across the clearing. The fairy danced ahead of them, glowing like a crimson flame. She stopped at a small pond under a weeping willow tree. "Look! I can *show* you what happened yesterday," she said. Ruby flew over the pond and scattered another shower of sparkling fairy dust with her tiny, red wand.

All at once, the water lit up with a strange, silver light. It bubbled and fizzed, and then became still. With wide eyes, Rachel and Kirsty watched as a picture appeared in the water. It was like looking through a window into another land!

"Oh, Rachel, look!" said Kirsty.

A river of the brightest blue ran swiftly past hills of the greenest green. Scattered on the hillsides were red-and-white toadstool houses.

And on top of the highest hill stood a silver palace with four pink towers.

The towers were so high, their points were almost hidden by the fluffy white clouds that floated past.

Hundreds of fairies were making their way toward the palace. Some were walking and some were flying. Rachel and Kirsty could see goblins, elves, and pixies too. Everyone seemed very excited.

"Yesterday was the day of the Fairyland Midsummer Ball," Ruby explained. She flew over the pond and pointed with her wand at a spot in the middle of the scene. "There I am, with my Rainbow sisters."

Kirsty and Rachel looked closely at where Ruby was pointing. They saw seven fairies, each dressed prettily in their own rainbow color. Wherever they flew, they left a trail of fairy dust behind them.

"The Midsummer Ball is *very* special," Ruby went on. "And my sisters and I are always in charge of sending out invitations."

The front doors of the palace slowly opened to the sound of tinkling music.

"Here come King Oberon and Queen Titania," said Ruby. "The Fairy King and Queen. They are about to begin the ball."

Kirsty and Rachel watched as the king and queen stepped through the doors. The king wore a splendid golden coat and crown. His queen wore a silver

dress and a tiara that sparkled with diamonds.

Everyone cheered loudly. After a while, the king signaled for quiet. "Fairies and friends," he began. "We are very glad to see you all here. Welcome to the Midsummer Ball!"

The fairies clapped their hands and cheered again. A band of green frogs in purple suits started to play their instruments, and the dancing began.

Suddenly, a gray mist filled the room. Kirsty and Rachel watched in alarm as all the fairies started to shiver.

Then a loud, chilly voice shouted out,
"Stop the music!"

The band fell silent. Everyone looked
scared. A tall, bony figure was pushing his
way through the crowd. He was dressed all
in white, and there were tiny icicles on his
white hair and beard. But his face
was red and angry.

"Who's that?" Rachel asked with a shiver. Ice had begun to form around the edge of the pond.

"It's Jack Frost," said Ruby. And she shivered, too.

In the watery picture Jack Frost glared at the seven Rainbow Fairies. "Why wasn't I invited to the Midsummer Ball?" he asked coldly.

The Rainbow Fairies gasped in horror . . .

Ruby looked up and smiled sadly at Rachel and Kirsty. "Yes, we forgot to invite Jack Frost," she said, and looked back at the pond.

They watched as the Fairy Queen stepped forward. "You are more than welcome, Jack Frost," she said. "Please stay and enjoy the ball."

But Jack Frost looked even more angry. "Too late!" he hissed. "You forgot to invite me!" He turned and pointed a thin, icy finger at the Rainbow Fairies.

"Well, you will not forget this!" he went on. "My spell will banish the Rainbow Fairies to the seven corners of the human world. From this day on, Fairyland will be without color—forever!"

JACK FROST'S SPELL

As Rachel and Kirsty kept watching the pond's surface, they saw Jack Frost cast his spell. A great, icy wind began to blow. It picked up the seven Rainbow Fairies and spun them up into the darkening sky. The other fairies could only watch in dismay.

Jack Frost turned to the king and queen. "Your Rainbow Fairies will be trapped, far away. They will be all alone, and they will never return." With that, he left, leaving only a trail of icy footprints behind.

Quickly, the Fairy Queen stepped forward and lifted her silver wand. "Jack Frost's magic is very powerful. I cannot undo it completely," she shouted, as the wind howled and rushed around her. "But I can guide the Rainbow Fairies to a place where they will be safe until they are rescued!"

The queen pointed her wand at the gray sky overhead. A black pot came spinning through the stormy clouds. It flew toward the Rainbow Fairies. One by one, the Rainbow Fairies tumbled into the pot.

"May this pot at the end of the rainbow keep our Rainbow Fairies together and safe," the queen called. "And take them to Rainspell Island!"

As Rachel, Kirsty, and Ruby watched,
the pot flew out of sight. It disappeared
behind a dark cloud. And the bright
colors of Fairyland began to fade, until
the beautiful land looked like an old
black-and-white photograph.

"Oh no!" Kirsty gasped. "All the
color is gone." Then the picture in the
pond vanished.

"So the Fairy Queen cast her *own*
spell!" Rachel said. She was bursting
with questions. "She put you and
your sisters in the pot, and sent you to
Rainspell Island?"

Ruby nodded. "Our queen knew that
we would be safe here," she said. "We
know Rainspell well. It is a place full
of magic."

"But where are your sisters?" Kirsty

asked. "They were in the pot, too."

Ruby looked upset. "Jack Frost's magic was very strong," she said. "The wind from his spell blew my sisters right out of the pot. We were still spinning through the sky, and all at once they were gone." Ruby shook her head. "I was at the bottom, so I was safe. But I was trapped when the pot landed upside down. In the dark, I was frightened and alone. My fairy magic wouldn't even work!"

"So are your sisters somewhere on Rainspell?" Kirsty asked.

Ruby nodded. "Yes, but they're scattered all over the island. I'm sure Jack Frost's spell has trapped them, too." She flew toward Kirsty and landed on her shoulder. "That's where you and Rachel come in."

"How?" Rachel asked.

"You found *me*, didn't you?" the fairy went on. "That's because you believe in magic." She flew from Kirsty's shoulder to Rachel's. "So, you could rescue my Rainbow sisters, too! Once we're together, we can bring color back to Fairyland again."

A VISIT TO FAIRYLAND

"Of course we'll search for your sisters,"
Kirsty said quickly. "Won't we, Rachel?"

Rachel nodded.

"Oh, thank you," Ruby said happily.

"But we're only here for a week,"
Rachel said. "Will that be long enough?"

"We must get started right away,"
said Ruby. "First, I must take you to

Fairyland to meet our king and queen.
They will be very pleased to know
that you are going to help me find my
sisters."

Rachel and Kirsty stared at Ruby.

"You're taking us to *Fairyland*?" Kirsty
gasped. She could hardly believe her ears.

"But how will we get there?" Rachel
wanted to know.

"We'll fly," Ruby replied.

"But *we* can't fly!" Rachel pointed out.

Ruby smiled. She whirled up into
the air over the girls' heads. Then she
swirled her wand above them. Magic red
fairy dust fluttered down.

Rachel and Kirsty began to feel a bit
strange. Were the trees getting bigger or
were they getting smaller?

They were getting *smaller*!
Rachel and Kirsty got smaller
and smaller, until they were
the same size as Ruby.

"I'm tiny!" Rachel
laughed. She was so small, the
flowers around her seemed as
big as trees.

Kirsty twisted around to look at her
back. She had wings—
shiny and delicate as
a butterfly's!
Ruby beamed
at them. "Now
you can fly," she
said. "Let's go."

Rachel twitched her shoulders. Her wings fluttered, and she rose up into the air. She felt very wobbly at first. Flying was not at all like walking!

"Help!" Kirsty yelled, as she shot up into the air. "I'm not very good at this!"

"Come on," said Ruby, taking their hands. "I'll help you." She led them up, out of the meadow.

From the air, Rachel looked down on Rainspell Island. She could see the cottages next to the beach, and the harbor.

"Where *is* Fairyland, Ruby?" Kirsty asked. They were flying higher and higher, up into the clouds.

"It's so far away that no human could ever find it," Ruby said.

They flew on through the clouds for a long, long time. But at last Ruby turned to them and smiled. "We're here," she said. "Luckily, while we're in Fairyland, no time passes in your world. No one will even know you were gone!"

As they flew down from the clouds, Kirsty and Rachel saw places they recognized from the pond picture: the palace, the hillsides with their toadstool houses, and the river. But there were no bright colors now. Because of Jack Frost's spell, everything was a drab shade of gray.

A few fairies walked miserably across the hillsides. Their wings hung limply down their backs.

No one even had the energy to fly.

Suddenly, one of the fairies glanced up into the sky. "Look!" she shouted. "It's Ruby. She's come back!"

At once, the fairies flew up toward Ruby, Kirsty, and Rachel.

They circled around Ruby, looking
much happier, and asking lots of questions.

"Where are the other Rainbow Fairies?"
"Who are your friends?"
"First, we must see the king and queen.
Then I will tell you everything!" Ruby
promised.
King Oberon and Queen Titania were
seated on their thrones. Their palace was

as gray and gloomy as everywhere else in Fairyland. But they smiled warmly when Ruby arrived with Rachel and Kirsty.

"Welcome back, Ruby," the queen said. "We have missed you."

"Your Majesties, I have found two humans who believe in magic!" Ruby announced. "These are my friends, Kirsty and Rachel."

Quickly, Ruby explained what had happened to the other Rainbow Fairies. She told everyone how Rachel and Kirsty had rescued her.

"You have our thanks," the king told them. "Our Rainbow Fairies are very special to us."

"And will you help us find Ruby's Rainbow sisters?" the queen asked.

"Yes, we will," Kirsty said.

"But how will we know where to look?" Rachel asked.

"The trick is not to look too hard," said Queen Titania. "Don't worry. As you enjoy the rest of your vacation, the magic you need to find each Rainbow Fairy will find *you*. Just wait and see."

King Oberon rubbed his beard thoughtfully. "You have six days of your vacation left, and six fairies to find," he said. "A fairy each day. That's a lot of fairy-finding. You will need some special help." He nodded at one of his footmen, a plump frog in a buttoned-up jacket.

The frog hopped over to Rachel and Kirsty and handed them each a tiny, silver bag.

"The bags contain magic tools," the queen told them. "Don't look inside them yet. Open them only when you really need to, and you will find something to help you." She smiled at Kirsty and Rachel.

"Look!" shouted another frog footman suddenly. "Ruby is beginning to fade!"

Rachel and Kirsty looked at Ruby in horror. The fairy was growing paler before their eyes. Her beautiful dress was no longer red, but pink, and her golden hair was turning white.

"Jack Frost's magic is still at work," said the king, looking worried. "We cannot undo his spell until the Rainbow Fairies are all together again."

"Quickly, Ruby!" urged the queen. "You must return to Rainspell at once."

Ruby, Kirsty, and Rachel rose into the air, their wings fluttering.

"Don't worry!" Kirsty called, as they flew higher. "We'll be back with all the Rainbow Fairies very soon!"

"Good luck!" called the king and queen.

Rachel and Kirsty watched Ruby worriedly as they flew off together. As they got farther away from Fairyland, Ruby's color began to return. Soon she was bright and sparkling again.

The three girls reached Rainspell at last.
Ruby led Rachel and Kirsty to the
clearing in the woods, and
they landed next to the
old, black pot. Then
Ruby scattered fairy
dust over Rachel
and Kirsty.
There was a puff
of glittering red
smoke, and the
two girls shot up
to their normal
size again.
Rachel wriggled
her shoulders. Yes,
her wings were gone.
"Oh, I really *loved*
being a fairy," Kirsty said.

They watched as Ruby sprinkled her magic dust over the old, black pot.

"What are you doing?" Rachel asked.

"Jack Frost's magic means that I can't help you look for my sisters," Ruby replied sadly. "If I try, I might fade away completely. So I will wait for you here, in the pot at the end of the rainbow."

Suddenly, the pot began to move. It rolled across the grass, and stopped under the weeping willow tree. The tree's branches hung right down to the ground.

"The pot will be hidden under that tree," Ruby explained. "I'll be safe there."

"We'd better start looking for the other Rainbow Fairies," Rachel said to Kirsty. "Where should we start?"

Ruby shook her head. "Remember what the queen said," she told them. "The magic will come to you." She flew over and sat on the edge of the pot. Then she pushed aside one of the willow branches and waved at Rachel and Kirsty. "Good-bye, and good luck!"

"We'll be back soon, Ruby," Kirsty promised.

"We're going to find all of your Rainbow sisters," Rachel said firmly.

"Just you wait and see!"

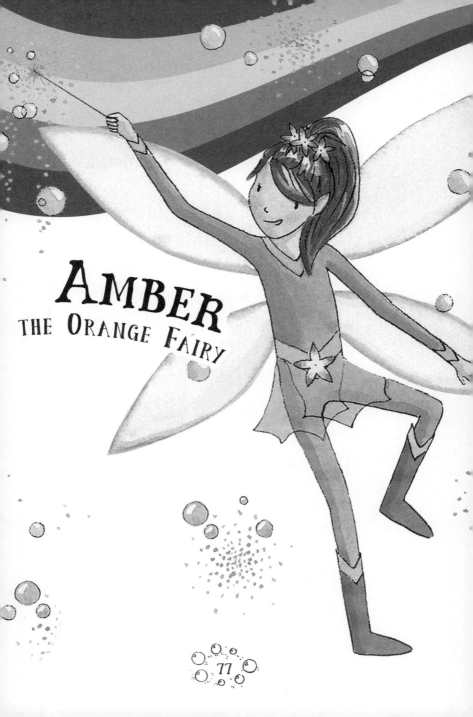

AMBER
THE ORANGE FAIRY

COLD WINDS BLOW AND THICK ICE FORM,
I CONJURE UP THIS FAIRY STORM.
TO SEVEN CORNERS OF THE HUMAN WORLD
THE RAINBOW FAIRIES WILL BE HURLED!

I CURSE EVERY PART OF FAIRYLAND,
WITH A FROSTY WAVE OF MY ICY HAND.
FOR NOW AND ALWAYS, FROM THIS DAY,
FAIRYLAND WILL BE COLD AND GRAY!

Ruby is safely hidden in the pot at the end of the rainbow. Now Rachel and Kirsty must find

AMBER THE ORANGE FAIRY.

Table of Contents

A Very Unusual Shell

"What a beautiful day!" Rachel Walker shouted, staring up at the blue sky. She and her friend Kirsty Tate were running along Rainspell Island's yellow, sandy beach. Their parents walked a little way behind them.

"It's a *magical* day," Kirsty added. The two friends smiled at each other.

Rachel and Kirsty had come to
Rainspell Island for their vacations.
But they soon found out it really *was* a
magical place!

As they ran, they passed tide pools that
sparkled like jewels in the sunshine.

Rachel spotted a little *splash!* in one of
the pools. "There's something in there,
Kirsty!" She pointed. "Let's go look."

The girls jogged over to the pool and
crouched down to see.

Kirsty's heart thumped as she gazed into the crystal-clear water. "What is it?" she asked.

Suddenly, the water rippled. A little brown crab scuttled sideways across the sandy bottom and disappeared under a rock.

Kirsty felt disappointed. "I thought it might be another Rainbow Fairy," she said.

"So did I." Rachel sighed. "Never mind. We'll keep looking."

"Of course we will," Kirsty agreed. Then she put her finger to her lips as their parents came up behind them. "*Shhh.*"

Kirsty and Rachel had a big secret. They were helping to find the seven missing Rainbow Fairies. Jack Frost put a wicked spell on the fairies and trapped them on Rainspell Island. The Rainbow Fairies made Fairyland bright and colorful. Until they were all found, Fairyland would be dark and gray.

Rachel looked at the shimmering blue sea. "Do you want to go swimming?" she asked.

But Kirsty wasn't listening. She was shading her eyes with her hand and looking farther along the beach. "Look over there, Rachel—by those rocks," she said.

Then Rachel could see it too—something glittering and sparkling in the sunshine. "Wait for me!" she called, as Kirsty hurried down the beach.

When they saw what it was, the two friends sighed in disappointment.

"It's just the wrapper from a chocolate bar," Rachel said sadly. She bent down and picked up the shiny purple foil.

Kirsty thought for a moment. "Do you remember what the Fairy Queen told us?" she asked.

Rachel nodded. "*Let the magic come to you*," she said. "You're right, Kirsty. We should just enjoy our vacation, and wait for the magic to happen. After all, that's how we found Ruby in the pot at the end of the rainbow, isn't it?" She put her beach bag down on the sand. "Come on—race you into the water!"

They rushed into the water. The sea was cold
and salty, but the sun felt warm on their backs.
They waved at their parents, sitting on the
sand, and splashed around in the waves until
they got goose bumps.

"Ow!" Kirsty gasped as
they paddled out of the
water. "I just stepped on
something sharp."

"It might have been
a shell," said Rachel.
"There are lots of them
around here." She picked
up a pale pink one and
showed it to Kirsty.

"Let's see how many we can
find," Kirsty said.

The two girls walked along the beach looking
for shells. They found long, thin, blue shells
and tiny, round, white shells.

Soon their hands were full.
They had walked right
around the curve of
the bay.
Rachel looked over
her shoulder and a
sudden gust of wind
whipped her hair
across her face.
"Look how far
we've come," she
said. Kirsty stopped.
The wind blew at
her back and made
goose bumps stand
out on her arms.
"It's getting cold
now," she said.
"Should we go back?"

"Yes, it must be almost lunchtime," said Rachel.

The two girls began to walk back along the beach. They'd only gone a few steps when the wind suddenly stopped.

"That's funny," said Kirsty. "It's not windy here at all."

They looked back and saw perfect little swirls of sand being lifted by the wind. "Oh!" said Rachel, and the two friends looked at each other in excitement.

"It's magic," Kirsty whispered. "It just *has* to be!"

They walked back to where they had
been, and the breeze swirled around their
legs again. Then the golden sand at their
feet began to drift gently to one side, as
if invisible hands were pushing it away.
A large scallop shell appeared. It was
much bigger than the other shells on the
beach. It was a light peach color with soft
orange streaks, and it was tightly closed.

Quickly the girls kneeled down on the sand, dropping the little shells from their hands. Kirsty was just about to pick up the scallop shell when Rachel put out her hand. "Listen," she whispered.

They both listened hard.

Rachel smiled when she heard the sound again.

Inside the shell, a tiny voice hummed softly . . .

THE MAGIC FEATHER

Very carefully, Rachel picked up the shell. It felt warm and smooth.

The humming stopped at once. "I should not be scared," said the tiny voice. "I just have to be brave, and help will come very soon."

Hummm...

Kirsty put her face close to the shell. "Hello," she whispered. "Is there a fairy in there?"

"Yes!" cried the voice. "I'm Amber the Orange Fairy! Can you get me out of here?"

"Of course we will," Kirsty promised. "My name is Kirsty, and my friend Rachel is here, too." She looked up at Rachel, her eyes shining. "We've found another Rainbow Fairy!"

"Quick," Rachel said. "Let's get the shell open." She took hold of the scallop shell and tried to pull the two halves apart. Nothing happened.

"Try again," said
Kirsty. She and Rachel
each grasped one half
of the shell and tugged.
But the shell stayed
tightly shut.

"What's happening?"
Amber called. She sounded worried.

"We can't open the shell," Kirsty said.
"But we'll think of something." She
turned to Rachel. "If we find a piece of
driftwood, maybe we could use it to
open the shell."

Rachel glanced around the beach.
"I don't see any driftwood," she said.
"We could try tapping the shell
on a rock."

"But that might hurt Amber," Kirsty
pointed out.

Suddenly, Rachel remembered something. "What about the magic bags the Fairy Queen gave us?" she said.

"Of course!" Kirsty cried. She put her face close to the shell again. "Amber, we're going to look in our magic bags," she said.

"OK, but please hurry," Amber called. Rachel opened her beach bag. The two magic bags were hidden under her towel. One of the bags was glowing with a golden light.

Carefully, Rachel pulled it out.

"Look," she whispered to Kirsty. "This one is all lit up."

"Open it, quick," Kirsty whispered back.

Kirsty and Rachel stared at the feather. "It's really pretty," said Kirsty. "But what are we going to *do* with it?"

"I don't know," Rachel replied. She tried to use the feather to push the two halves of the shell apart. But the feather just curled up in her hand. "Maybe we should ask Amber."

"Amber, we've looked in the magic bags," Kirsty said, "and we've found a feather."

"Oh, good!" Amber said happily from inside the shell. "That's wonderful news!"

"But we don't know what to do with it," Rachel added.

Amber laughed. It sounded like the tinkle of a tiny bell. "You tickle the shell, of course!" she said.

"Do you think that will work?" Rachel said to Kirsty.

"Let's give it a try," Kirsty said.

Rachel began to tickle the shell with the feather. At first nothing happened. Then they heard a soft, gritty chuckle, followed by a tinkly giggle from inside the shell. Then another chuckle, and another. Slowly, the two halves of the shell began to open.

"It's working," Kirsty gasped. "Keep tickling, Rachel!"

The shell was laughing hard now. The two halves opened wider . . .

And there, sitting inside the smooth, peach-colored shell, was Amber the Orange Fairy.

A STRANGER IN THE POT

"I'm free!" Amber cried joyfully.

She shot out of the shell and up into
the air, her wings fluttering in a rainbow-
colored blur. Orange fairy dust floated
down around Kirsty and Rachel. It turned
into orange bubbles as it fell. One of the
bubbles landed on Rachel's arm and burst
with a tiny *pop*!

"The bubbles smell like oranges!"
Rachel said with a smile.

Amber spun through the sky, turning
cartwheels one after the other. "Thank
you!" she called. Then she swooped
down toward Rachel and Kirsty.

She wore a shiny orange leotard and
tall boots. Her brown hair was held in a
high ponytail, tied with a band of peach
blossoms. In her hand was an orange
wand tipped with gold.

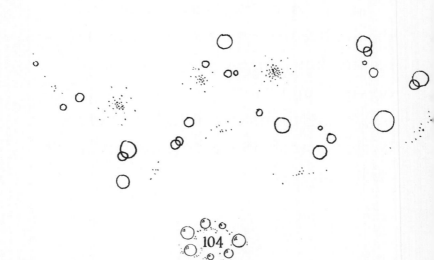

"I'm so glad you found me!" Amber shouted. She landed on Rachel's shoulder, then cartwheeled lightly across to Kirsty's. "But who are you? And where are my Rainbow sisters? And what's happening in Fairyland? How am I going to get back there?"

She was talking so fast that Kirsty and Rachel couldn't get a word in.

Suddenly, Amber stopped. She floated
down and landed softly on Rachel's hand.
"I'm sorry," she said with a smile. "But I
haven't had anyone to talk to. I've been shut
up in that shell ever since Jack Frost's spell
banished us from Fairyland. How did you
know where to find me?"

"Kirsty and I promised your sister Ruby
that we would look for all the Rainbow
Fairies," Rachel told her.

"Ruby?" Amber's face lit up. She spun
around on Rachel's hand. "You've found
Ruby?"

"Yes, she's safe now," Rachel said. "She's
in the pot at the end of the rainbow."

Amber did a happy backflip. "Please take
me to her!" she begged.

"I'll ask our parents if we can go for a
walk," Kirsty said. And she ran off across
the beach.

"Do you know what is
happening in Fairyland?"
Amber asked Rachel.

Rachel nodded.
She and Kirsty had
flown with Ruby to
Fairyland. Ruby had
used her wand to
shrink them to fairy
size, and she had
given them magical
fairy wings. "King
Oberon and Queen
Titania miss you
very much," Rachel
told Amber. "With
no color, Fairyland
is a sad place."

Kirsty was hurrying back toward
them. "Mom said we can go for a
walk," she panted.

"Well, what are we waiting for? Let's
go!" Amber called. She flew up and
did a somersault in midair.

Rachel pulled their
shorts, T-shirts, and
sneakers out of her
beach bag and both
girls put them on.

"Rachel, could
you bring my
shell?" Amber asked.
Rachel looked surprised.

"Yes, if you want," she said.

Amber nodded. "It's really comfy,"
she explained. "It will make a nice bed
for me and my sisters."

Rachel put the shell in her beach bag
and they set off with Amber sitting cross-
legged on Kirsty's shoulder.

"My wings are a bit stiff after being in
the shell," she told them. "I don't think I
can fly very far yet."

The girls followed the path to the clearing in the woods where the pot at the end of the rainbow was hidden.

"Here we are," said Rachel. "The pot is right over there." She stopped. The pot was where they'd left it—under the weeping willow tree. But climbing out of it was a big, green frog.

"Oh no!" Rachel gasped. She and Kirsty stared at the frog in horror.

Where was Ruby?

Home Sweet Home

Rachel dashed forward and grabbed the frog around his plump, green belly.

The frog turned his head and glared at her, his eyes bulging. "And what do you think *you're* doing?" he croaked.

Rachel was so shocked, she let go of the frog. He hopped away from her, looking very annoyed.

"It's a talking frog!" Kirsty gasped, her eyes wide. "And it looks like it's wearing glasses . . ."

"Bertram!" Amber flew down from Kirsty's shoulder. "I didn't know it was you."

Bertram bowed his head as Amber hugged him. "Thank goodness you're safe, Miss Amber!" he said happily. "And may I say, it's very good to see you again."

Amber beamed at Rachel and Kirsty. "Bertram isn't an ordinary frog, you know," she explained. "He's one of King Oberon's footmen. He works closely with the king and queen."

"Oh, yes!" said Kirsty. "I remember now. We saw the frog footmen when we went to Fairyland with Ruby."

"But they were wearing uniforms then," Rachel added.

"Excuse me, Miss, but a frog in a uniform would *not* be a good idea on Rainspell Island," Bertram pointed out. "It's much better if I look like an ordinary frog."

"But what are you doing here, Bertram?" asked Amber. "And where's Ruby?"

"Don't worry, Miss Amber," Bertram replied. "Miss Ruby is safe in the pot." He suddenly looked very stern. "King Oberon sent me to Rainspell. The Cloud Fairies spotted Jack Frost's goblins sneaking out of Fairyland. We think he has sent them here to stop you from finding the Rainbow Fairies."

Kirsty felt a shiver run down her spine. "Jack Frost's goblins?" she said.

"They're his servants," Amber explained. Her wings trembled and she looked very scared. "They want to keep Fairyland cold and gray!"

"Never fear, Miss Amber," Bertram croaked. "I'm here to look after you and keep the Rainbow Fairies safe."

Suddenly, a shower of red fairy dust shot out of the pot. Ruby fluttered out. "I heard voices," she shouted joyfully. "Amber! I *knew* it was you!"

"Ruby!" Amber called. And then she cartwheeled through the air toward her sister.

Rachel and Kirsty watched as the two fairies flew into each other's arms. The air around them fizzed with little red flowers and orange bubbles.

"Thank you, Kirsty and Rachel," said
Ruby. She and Amber floated down to
them, holding hands. "It's so good to
have Amber back safely."

"What about you?"
Rachel asked. "Have you
been OK in the pot?"

Ruby nodded. "I'm
fine now that Bertram is
here," she replied. "And
I've been making the pot into
a fairy home. We can stay there until all
our fairy sisters are found."

"I brought my shell with me," Amber
said. "It will make a nice bed for us.
Could you show her, Rachel?"

Rachel put her bag down on the
grass and took the peach-colored shell
out of it.

"It's beautiful," said Ruby. Then she smiled at Rachel and Kirsty. "Would you like to come and see our new home?" she asked.

"But the pot's too small for Kirsty and me to fit inside," Rachel began. Then she began to tingle with excitement. "Oh! Are you going to make us fairy size again?"

Ruby nodded. She and Amber flew over the girls' heads, showering them with fairy dust. Rachel and Kirsty started to shrink, just as they had before. Soon they were the same size as Ruby and Amber.

"I *love* being a fairy," Kirsty said happily. She twisted around to look at her silvery wings.

"Me too," Rachel agreed. She was getting used to seeing flowers as tall as trees!

Bertram hopped over to the pot. "I'll wait outside," he croaked.

"Come this way," said Ruby. She took Rachel's hand, and Amber took Kirsty's. Then the fairies led them toward the pot.

Rachel and Kirsty fluttered through the air, dodging a butterfly that was as big as they were. Its wings felt like velvet as they brushed gently past it.

"I'm getting better at flying!" Kirsty laughed as she landed neatly on the edge of the pot. She looked down eagerly.

The pot was full of sunlight. There were little chairs made from twigs tied with blades of grass. Each chair had a cushion made from a soft red berry. Rugs of bright green leaves covered the floor.

"Should we bring in the shell?" asked Rachel.
The others thought this was a very good idea.
When they flew out of the pot, Bertram was
already pushing the shell across the grass toward
them.

"Here you are," he croaked.

The shell seemed very heavy now that Rachel and Kirsty were the same size as Ruby and Amber. But Bertram helped them to lift it into the pot.

Soon the shell bed sat neatly inside. Ruby lined it with sweet-smelling rose petals.

"The pot looks beautiful," Rachel said.

"I wish I could live here, too!" said Kirsty.

Ruby turned to her sister. "Do you like it, Amber?" she asked.

"It's beautiful," Amber replied. "It reminds me of our house back in Fairyland. I wish I could see Fairyland again. I miss it so much."

Ruby smiled. "Well, we can't go back to Fairyland for good until we're all together," she explained. "But I can *show* you Fairyland. Follow me!"

Bertram was still on guard next to the pot when they flew outside again. "Where are you going, Miss Ruby?" he croaked.

"To the magic pond," Ruby replied. "Come with us." She sprinkled her magic dust over Rachel and Kirsty. Quickly, they grew back to their normal size.

They went over to the pond.
Ruby flew above the
water, scattering
fairy dust. Just like
before, a picture
began to appear.
"Fairyland!" Amber
cried, gazing into the water.
Rachel and Kirsty watched too.

Fairyland still looked
sad and chilly.
The palace, the
toadstool houses,
flowers, and the
trees were all icy
and gray.

Suddenly, a cold breeze rippled the
surface of the water, and the picture
began to fade.

"What's happening?" Kirsty whispered.
Everyone stared down at the pond.

Another picture was taking shape—a
thin, grinning face with frosty white hair,
and icicles hanging from his beard.

"Jack Frost!" Ruby gasped in horror.
As she spoke, the air turned icy cold and
the edges of the pool began to freeze.

"What's happening?" Rachel asked, shivering.

Bertram hopped forward. "This is bad news," he said. "It means that Jack Frost's goblins must be close by!"

GOBLIN ALERT!

Rachel and Kirsty felt shivers run down their spines as the whole pond froze over. Jack Frost's grinning face faded away.

"Follow me," ordered Bertram. He hopped over to a large bush. "We'll hide here."

"Maybe we should go back to the pot," said Ruby.

"Not if the goblins are close by," Bertram replied. "We can't let them know where the pot is."

The two girls crouched behind the bush next to Bertram. Ruby and Amber sat very still on Kirsty's shoulder. It was getting colder and colder. Rachel and Kirsty couldn't stop their teeth from chattering.

"What are the goblins like?" Rachel asked.

"They're bigger than we are," said Amber. She was trembling with fright.

"And they have mean faces and long noses and big feet," Ruby added, holding her sister's hand for comfort.

"Hush, Miss Ruby," Bertram croaked. "I can hear something."

Rachel and Kirsty listened. Suddenly, Rachel saw a long-nosed shadow dash across the clearing toward them. She grabbed Kirsty's arm. They were peering out of the bush when the leaves rustled right next to them. They almost jumped out of their skin.

"Hey!" said a gruff voice, sounding very close. "What do you think you're doing?" Rachel and Kirsty held their breath.

"Nothing," said another gruff voice.

"Goblins!" Amber whispered in Kirsty's ear.

"You stepped on my toe," said the first goblin angrily.

"No, I didn't," snapped the other goblin.

"Yes, you did! Keep your big feet to yourself!"

"Well, at least my nose isn't as big as yours!"

The bush shook. It sounded as if the goblins were pushing and shoving each other.

"Get out of my way!" one of them shouted. "Ow!"

"That'll teach you to push *me*!" yelled the other one.

Rachel and Kirsty looked at each other in alarm. What if the goblins found them there?

"Come on," puffed one of the goblins.
"Jack Frost will be really angry if we
don't find these fairies. You know he
wants us to keep them from getting back
to Fairyland."

"Well, they're not here, are they?"
grumbled the other. "Let's try
somewhere else."

The voices died away. The leaves
stopped rustling. Suddenly, the air felt
warm again. There was a cracking sound
as the frozen pond began to melt.

"They're gone," Bertram croaked.
"Quick, we must get back to the pot."

They all hurried across the clearing.
The pot stood under the weeping willow
tree, just as before.

"I'll stay outside in case the goblins come back," Bertram began. But a shout from Kirsty stopped them all in their tracks.

"Look!" she cried. "The pot's frozen over!"

Kirsty was right. The top of the pot was covered with a thick sheet of ice. No one, not even a fairy, could get inside.

BERTRAM TO THE RESCUE

"Oh no!" Ruby gasped. "The goblins must have been really close. Thank goodness they didn't discover the pot."

She flew over to the pot with Amber right behind her. They drummed on the ice with their tiny fists. But it was too thick for them to break through.

"Should *we* try, Rachel?" asked
Kirsty. "Maybe we could smash the ice
with a stick."

But Bertram had another idea. "Stand
back, please, everyone," he said.

The girls moved to the edge of the
clearing. Ruby sat on Kirsty's hand,
and Amber flew over to Rachel. They
all watched.

Suddenly, Bertram leaped forward
with a mighty hop. He
jumped straight at
the sheet of ice,
kicking out with
his webbed feet.
But the ice did
not break.
"Let's try again,"
he panted.

He jumped forward again and hit the ice. This time, there was a loud cracking sound. After one more jump, the ice shattered into little pieces. Some of it fell inside the pot. Rachel and Kirsty rushed over to fish out the pieces of ice before they melted.

"There you are," Bertram croaked.

"Thank you, Bertram," Ruby called. She and Amber flew down and hugged the frog.

Bertram looked pleased. "Just doing my job, Miss Ruby," he said. "You and Miss Amber must stay very close to the pot from now on. It's dangerous for you to go too far."

"We have to say good-
bye to our friends first,"
Amber told him. She flew
into the air and did a
backflip, smiling at Rachel
and Kirsty. "Thank you a
thousand times."

"We'll see you again soon,"
said Rachel.

"When we've found your next
Rainbow sister," Kirsty added.

"Good luck!" said Ruby. "We'll be
waiting here for you. Come on, Amber."

She took her sister's hand, and
they flew over to the pot.
The two fairies turned to
wave at the girls. Then they
disappeared inside.

"Don't worry," Bertram said. "I'll look after them."

"We know you will," Rachel said, as she picked up her beach bag. She and Kirsty walked out of the woods. "I'm glad Ruby isn't on her own anymore," said Rachel. "Now she has Amber *and* Bertram."

"I didn't like those goblins," Kirsty said with a shudder. "I hope they don't come back again."

The girls made their way back to the beach. Their parents were packing up their towels. Rachel's dad saw Rachel and Kirsty coming down the path and went to meet them. "You've been gone a long time," he smiled. "We were just coming to look for you."

"Are we going back to the cottage now?" Rachel asked.

Mr. Walker nodded. "It's very strange," he said. "It's suddenly turned quite chilly."

As he spoke, a cold breeze swirled around Rachel and Kirsty. They shivered and looked up at the sky. The sun had disappeared behind a thick, black cloud. The trees swayed in the wind, and the leaves rustled as if they were whispering to one another.

"Jack Frost's goblins are still here!" Kirsty gasped.

"You're right," Rachel agreed. "Let's hope Bertram can keep Ruby and Amber safe while we look for the other Rainbow Fairies."

Kirsty nodded and smiled at Rachel. They still had five fairies to find. It would take some magic and a lot of work, but she was sure they could do it together!

SUNNY
THE YELLOW FAIRY

COLD WINDS BLOW AND THICK ICE FORM,
I CONJURE UP THIS FAIRY STORM.
TO SEVEN CORNERS OF THE HUMAN WORLD
THE RAINBOW FAIRIES WILL BE HURLED!

I CURSE EVERY PART OF FAIRYLAND,
WITH A FROSTY WAVE OF MY ICY HAND.
FOR NOW AND ALWAYS, FROM THIS DAY,
FAIRYLAND WILL BE COLD AND GRAY!

Ruby and Amber have been rescued.

Now it's time to search for

SUNNY THE YELLOW FAIRY.

Table of Contents

A VERY BIG BEE

"Over here, Kirsty!" called Rachel
Walker. Kirsty Tate ran across one of the
emerald-green fields that covered this part
of Rainspell Island. Buttercups and daisies
dotted the grass.

"Don't go too far!" Kirsty's mom called.
She and Kirsty's dad were climbing over a
fence at the top of the field.

Kirsty caught up with her friend. "What did you find, Rachel? Is it another Rainbow Fairy?" she asked hopefully.

"I don't know." Rachel was standing on the bank of a rippling stream. "I thought I heard something."

Kirsty's face lit up. "Maybe there's a fairy in the stream?"

Rachel nodded. She knelt down on the soft grass and put her ear close to the water.

Kirsty crouched down too, and listened really hard.

The sun glittered on the water as it splashed over big, shiny pebbles. Tiny rainbows flashed and sparkled—red, orange, yellow, green, blue, indigo, and violet.

And then the girls heard a tiny bubbling voice. "Follow me . . ." it gurgled. "Follow me . . ."

"Oh!" Rachel gasped. "Did you hear that?"

"Yes," said Kirsty, her eyes wide. "It must be a *magic* stream!"

Rachel's heart beat fast. "Maybe the stream will lead us to the Yellow Fairy," she said.

Rachel and Kirsty had a special secret. They had promised the King and Queen of Fairyland they would find the lost Rainbow Fairies. Jack Frost's spell had hidden the Rainbow Fairies on Rainspell Island. Fairyland would be cold and gray until all seven fairies had been found and returned to their home.

Silver fish darted in and out of the bright green weeds at the bottom of the stream. "Follow us, follow us . . ." they whispered in tinkling voices.

Rachel and Kirsty smiled at each other. Titania, the Fairy Queen, had said that the magic would find them!

Kirsty's parents came up behind the girls and stopped to admire the stream, too. "Which way now?" asked Mr. Tate. "You two seem to know where you're going."

"Let's go this way," Kirsty said, pointing along the bank.

A brilliant bluebird flew up from its perch on a twig. Butterflies as bright as jewels fluttered among the cattails.

"Everything on Rainspell Island is so beautiful," said Kirsty's mom. "I'm glad we still have five days of vacation left!"

Yes, Rachel thought, *and five Rainbow Fairies still to find: Sunny, Fern, Sky, Inky, and Heather!* Ruby the Red Fairy and Amber the Orange Fairy were already safe in the pot at the end of the rainbow.

The girls ran on ahead of Mr. and Mrs. Tate. As they followed the bubbling stream, the sun went behind a big, dark cloud.

A chilly breeze ruffled Kirsty's hair. She noticed that some of the leaves on the trees were turning brown, even though it wasn't autumn. Strange weather like that could only mean one thing.

"It looks like Jack Frost's goblins are still around," she warned Rachel. Whenever the goblins were nearby, everything turned frosty and cold.

Rachel shivered. "Horrible creatures! They'll do anything to stop the Rainbow Fairies from getting back to Fairyland."

The two friends stared anxiously up at the sky. But just then, the sun came out again, warming their shoulders. The girls smiled with relief and continued to follow the bubbling water.

The stream wound through a field covered with green clover. A herd of black and white cows was grazing at the water's edge. They looked up with their huge, brown eyes.

"Aren't they cute?" Kirsty said.

Suddenly, the cows tossed their heads and ran off toward the other end of the field.

Rachel and Kirsty looked at each other in surprise. What was going on?

Then they heard a loud buzzing noise. A small shape came whizzing through the air, straight toward them!

Rachel jumped. "It's a bee!" she gasped. "Run!" Kirsty cried. The cows had the right idea! Rachel tore through the meadow with Kirsty right next to her, their feet pounding the grass.

"Keep running, girls," called Mr. Tate, catching up with them. "That bee seems like it's following us!"

Rachel glanced back. The bee was huge, bigger than any bee she'd ever seen.

"In here, quick!" Mrs. Tate called from the side of the field. She pulled open a wooden gate.

They all ran through it, then stopped to catch their breath. Hopefully, they'd lost that bee—for good!

"I wonder who lives here?" Kirsty panted. They were standing in a beautiful yard. A path led up to a little cottage with yellow roses around the door.

A Very Big Bee

Just then, a very strange creature came out from behind some trees. It looked like an alien from outer space!

"Oh!" Rachel and Kirsty gasped.

The creature lifted its gloved hands and removed its white helmet to reveal . . . an old woman! She smiled at them.

"Sorry if I startled you," she said. "I do look a bit strange in my beekeeper's suit."

Rachel sighed in relief. It wasn't a space alien after all!

"I'm Mrs. Merry," the old woman went on.

"Hello," Rachel said. "I'm Rachel. This is my friend, Kirsty."

"And this is my mom and dad," Kirsty added.

Mr. and Mrs. Tate greeted Mrs. Merry. Then Mr. Tate ducked as the huge bee zoomed past his ear.

"Watch out!" he said. "It's back!"

"Oh, it's that hiveless queen again," said Mrs. Merry. She flapped her hand at the bee. "Go on, shoo!" Rachel watched it swoop over a low hedge and disappear.

"That bee chased us all

the way here. Why would she do that?"
Kirsty asked.

"I don't think she was chasing you, my
dear," said Mrs. Merry. "She was just
heading this way because she's looking
for a hive of her own. But all of my hives
already have queens."

"Well, thank goodness she's gone now!"
said Mrs. Tate.

"Since you're here, would you like to
try some of my honey?" Mrs. Merry asked.
Her blue eyes sparkled happily.

"Oh, yes please,"
said Rachel.

The others nodded,
and they followed Mrs.
Merry across the lawn
to a table covered with
rows of jars.

Each jar was filled with rich, golden honey. Rays of sunlight danced over the jars, making the honey glow.

"Here you are," said Mrs. Merry, spooning some honey onto a pretty, yellow plate.

"Thank you," Rachel said politely. She dipped her finger into the little pool of honey and popped it into her mouth. The honey was the most delicious thing she had ever tasted—sweet and smooth.

Then she felt it begin to tingle on her tongue. She looked over at Kirsty. "It tastes all fizzy!" she whispered.

Kirsty dipped her finger into the honey, too. "And look!" she said.

Rachel saw that the honey was twinkling with thousands of tiny, gold sparkles. She grabbed Kirsty's arm. "Do you think this means—"

"Yes," said Kirsty. Her eyes were shining. "Another Rainbow Fairy must be nearby!"

THE MAGIC HIVE

"We have to find out where this honey came from!" Rachel said excitedly.

"Yes," Kirsty agreed. "Mom? Can we stay here a bit longer, please?"

"As long as it's OK with Mrs. Merry," Kirsty's mom replied.

Mrs. Merry beamed. "Of course, they can stay," she said kindly.

Mr. and Mrs. Tate decided to continue their walk. "Make sure you come back to Dolphin Cottage by lunchtime," Kirsty's mom said. "And be careful!"

"We will," Kirsty promised.

"Come along then, girls." Mrs. Merry set off across the smooth, green lawn.

Rachel and Kirsty followed her down the garden to some old and twisted apple trees. Six wooden hives stood underneath.

Kirsty stared at the row of hives. "Which hive did the honey we tasted come from?" she asked.

Mrs. Merry looked pleased. "Did you enjoy it? The honey from that hive tastes especially good at the moment."

Rachel and Kirsty grinned at each other.

"I think we might know why," Rachel whispered to Kirsty.

"Yes," Kirsty agreed. "It could be fairy honey!"

"That's the one," Mrs. Merry said proudly, pointing to the very back of the yard. One hive stood there all alone, beneath the biggest apple tree.

As they walked toward the hive, the girls could hear a sleepy buzzing sound.

"The bees in this hive are very peaceful nowadays," said Mrs. Merry. "I've never known them to be so happy."

"Can we get a bit closer?" Rachel asked eagerly. She couldn't wait to find out if the hive held a magical secret!

Mrs. Merry looked thoughtful. "I think it's safe, with the bees so quiet," she decided. "But you better wear a hood like mine, just in case."

She went into a nearby shed and brought out two beekeepers' hoods. "Here you are."

Rachel and Kirsty pulled the hoods over their heads. It was a bit dark and stuffy inside, but they could see through the netting just fine.

They moved closer to the hive. The soft buzzing sounded almost like music.

"We need to open it and take a look,"
Kirsty whispered to Rachel.

Rachel nodded.

But they couldn't start searching for
the Yellow Fairy with Mrs. Merry there.
Ruby had warned them that no
grown-ups should see the fairies.

Suddenly, Kirsty had an idea. "Mrs.
Merry, may I have a drink of water,
please?" she asked.

"Of course you can, dear," Mrs. Merry
said. She went off toward the cottage.

The girls waited until Mrs. Merry
disappeared inside.

"Quick!" Kirsty spun around. "Let's
open the hive."

Rachel grasped one end of the lid.
Kirsty took hold of the other end. They
pulled hard, and the lid slowly came

172

loose with a squeaky sound. Strings of golden
honey stretched down from it.

"Watch out. It's very sticky," Rachel said.

The girls bent down and laid the heavy
wooden top carefully on the ground. Kirsty
wiped her fingers on the grass.

"Look!" Rachel whispered as she stood up.
Kirsty turned to see, and gasped.

A shower of sparkling gold dust shot up out of the hive. It hung in a soft cloud, shimmering and dancing in the sunlight. Fairy dust!

Rachel leaned over and peered down into the hive. A tiny girl was sitting cross-legged on a piece of honeycomb, in the middle of a golden sea of honey. A bee lay with its head in her lap while she combed its silky hair. Several other bees were waiting their turn, buzzing gently.

"Oh, Kirsty," Rachel whispered. "We've found another Rainbow Fairy!"

BEE FRIENDS

Rachel and Kirsty took off their hoods and stared down into the hive with excitement.

The fairy had bright yellow hair. She wore a necklace of golden raindrops and lots of sparkly golden bracelets. Her T-shirt and shorts were the color of buttercups. Her delicate wings sparkled with a thousand shimmering rainbows.

"Oh, thank you for finding me!"
the fairy said in a tinkling voice. "I'm
Sunny the Yellow Fairy."

Rachel and Kirsty
introduced themselves.
"We've met two
of your sisters
already—Ruby
and Amber,"
Kirsty added.
Sunny beamed
happily.
"You've found
Ruby and Amber?"
She stood up, gently
pushing the bee away.
"Yes. They're safe in the pot at the end
of the rainbow," Rachel said.

Sunny clapped her tiny hands. "I can't *wait* to see them again." Suddenly, she looked worried. "Have you seen any of Jack Frost's goblins near here?" she asked.

"No, not here," Kirsty said. "But there were some by the pot yesterday."

"We hid in a bush until they went away," Rachel explained.

"Goblins are scary," Sunny said in a trembling voice. "I've been safe from them here in the hive, with my bee friends."

Rachel felt very sorry for Sunny. "It's all right. King Oberon sent one of his frog footmen to look after you and your sisters."

Sunny cheered up. "I've been really worried about finding my sisters. Jack Frost's magic is so cold and strong."

"It won't be much longer," Kirsty said. "We are going to find Fern, Sky, Inky, and Heather too, aren't we, Rachel?"

"Yes. We promised," Rachel agreed.

"Oh, thank you!" Sunny said. She
threw out her arms and gave a shake of
her sparkling wings.

Fairy dust rose into the air and drifted
down around Rachel and Kirsty. Where
it landed, bright yellow butterflies
appeared, with tiny fluttering wings.

A large bee crawled out of one of the
waxy openings in the honeycomb next
to Sunny.

"This is my new friend, Queenie," said Sunny. She put her arms around the bee's neck and kissed the top of her furry head.

Queenie buzzed softly.

"She says hello," said Sunny.

"Hello, Queenie," Kirsty and Rachel said together.

Sunny picked up her tiny comb and began to comb Queenie's shiny hair. Another bee buzzed angrily.

"Don't worry, Petal, I'll comb your hair next," Sunny said.

Rachel and Kirsty looked at each other in dismay.

"What if Sunny wants to stay with Queenie and the other bees?" Kirsty whispered.

"Sunny, you have to come with us!" Rachel burst out. "Or Fairyland will never get its colors back! It will take all of the Rainbow sisters to undo Jack Frost's spell."

FORGETFUL FAIRY

"Yes, of course! We have to break Jack Frost's spell!" Sunny cried. She jumped to her feet and picked up her wand.

Suddenly, an icy wind swept by. Something crunched under Kirsty's feet. There was a small patch of frost on the grass.

Rachel shivered as something cold brushed against her cheek.

"A snowflake in summer? What's happening?" she cried.

"Jack Frost's goblins must be near," Kirsty said worriedly.

Sunny's tiny teeth chattered with cold. "Oh, no! If they find me, they will stop me from getting back to Fairyland!"

Kirsty looked at Rachel in alarm.
"Quick, we have to go!"

Rachel leaned down
and lifted the fairy
out of the beehive.

Sunny's golden
hair dripped
with honey.

"Oh my,
you're really
sticky," Rachel said.

Just then, Kirsty
spotted Mrs. Merry
coming out of her cottage.

"I forgot I asked for a drink," Kirsty
said. "What are we going to do?"

Rachel thought for a moment, then
dropped the fairy into the pocket of
her shorts.

Sunny gave a cry of dismay. "Hey! It's dark in here!" she complained.

"Sorry," Rachel whispered. "I'll get you out again in a minute, I promise."

Suddenly, Kirsty noticed the open hive. "We have to put the top back on before Mrs. Merry sees it!" she said.

She bent down and grasped the lid. Rachel helped lift it and they quickly put it into place, just as Mrs. Merry came through the trees.

"Here's your drink, dear," said

Mrs. Merry, holding out a glass to Kirsty. She had taken off her strange suit, and was carrying a shopping basket in her other hand.

"Thank you very much," Kirsty said, taking the glass.

"Now, you girls stay as long as you like," said Mrs. Merry. "I need to run out and buy some tuna for my cat. It's time for his lunch!"

Rachel watched Mrs. Merry go toward the garden gate. Then she slipped her hand into her pocket. "You can come out now," she said to Sunny, gently lifting her out.

The fairy was covered with gray fuzz from Rachel's pocket. "Achoo!" Sunny sneezed and brushed angrily at the bits of sticky fuzz clinging to her wings. "I'm all clogged up!" she wailed. "I won't be able to fly."

"We can help clean you up," Rachel said. "But we'll have to be quick, in case the goblins find us."

Kirsty looked around and spotted a
stone bird bath filled with clear water.
"Over there."

"Just what we need," Rachel agreed.
She carried Sunny over to the bird bath.

Sunny fluttered onto the
edge of the bath,
put down her
wand, and
dived in.

Splash!

The water
fizzed and
turned bright
yellow.
Lemony-
smelling drops
sprayed into the air.

Sunny swam two laps, and before long, she was sparkling clean. She zoomed up into the air to dry. Misty yellow trails appeared as she whooshed around. "That's better!" she cried.

She hovered in the air in front of Kirsty. Her wings flashed like gold in the sun. Then she swooped onto Rachel's shoulder. "Come on, let's go to the pot at the end of the rainbow!"

Rachel nodded. She wanted to leave the garden before the goblins got there.

"Good-bye, Queenie!" Sunny called, waving to her friend. "I'll come back to visit as soon as I can!"

Queenie peeked out of the hive. She seemed a bit sad that Sunny was leaving. Her feelers drooped as she waved a tiny leg and buzzed good-bye.

Sunny sat cross-legged on Rachel's shoulder as they headed for the woods. Suddenly, she cried out and flew up into the air. "Oh, no!" she gasped. "I left my wand next to the bird bath!"

Rachel looked at Kirsty with concern. "We'll have to go back," she said.

"Yes," Kirsty agreed. "We can't leave a fairy wand lying around for the goblins to find."

"Oh, dear . . . Oh, dear . . ."
Sunny zipped back and forth,
wringing her hands as they headed
back down the path.

Rachel paused at the gate and
looked into the garden. There was
no sign of goblins.

Kirsty and Rachel ran through
the apple trees, toward the birdbath.
Sunny fluttered just above them.

FORGETFUL FAIRY

Suddenly, an icy blast made them all shiver. They gazed around in alarm. Icicles now hung from the apple trees, and the whole lawn was white and crunchy with frost. The goblins had arrived! And they'd brought winter to the garden.

Sunny gave a cry of horror.

A big, large-nosed goblin jumped up on top of Queenie's hive. His bulging eyes gleamed. In one hand he was holding Sunny's wand!

WELL DONE, QUEENIE

"Give me back my wand!"
Sunny demanded.

"Come and get it!" yelled the
goblin rudely. He leaped off
the hive and ran toward
the gate.

Kirsty gasped as another
goblin jumped down from the
apple tree.

197

Crunch! He landed on the frosty grass and started to run.

"Catch!" The goblin threw the wand to his friend. It flew through the air, shooting out yellow sparks.

The other goblin reached up and caught the wand. "Hee, hee. Got it!"

"Oh, no!" Sunny gasped.

Just then, Queenie flew out of the hive with a loud buzz. All the other bees swarmed behind her in a noisy cloud.

Rachel watched, her eyes very wide. With Queenie in the lead, the bees formed into an arrow shape and raced after the goblins.

"Be careful, Queenie!" pleaded Sunny.

"Get away!" The goblin shook Sunny's wand at Queenie.

More bright yellow sparks shot out of the wand. One of the sparks hit Queenie's wing. Queenie wobbled in midair. Then she buzzed angrily and flew at the goblin again.

"Help!" The goblin ducked and dropped the wand.

"Butterfingers!" grumbled the other goblin, scooping it up and continuing to run.

"They're getting
away!" Kirsty cried.

Queenie and her
bees rose into the
air again.

"No, they're not!"
Rachel cried excitedly.

The bees shot across the yard and the
goblins disappeared in the angry swarm.

"Get off me!" sputtered the goblin
with the wand. He tried to shoo the
bees away, but tripped over his feet. As
he fell, he bumped into
the other goblin.

The two of them
tumbled over in
a heap, dropping
the wand onto
the grass.

"That was your fault!" complained one of the goblins.

"No, it wasn't!" snapped the other one.

Queenie zoomed over and picked up the wand with one of her tiny, black feet.

She carried it straight to Sunny, who was standing on Rachel's hand. With a little buzz, Queenie landed next to Sunny.

Sunny took her wand from Queenie and carefully waved it in the air.

A fountain of glittering
dust and fluttering
butterflies sparkled
around them.
"My wand is all right!"
Sunny cried joyfully.
"Look! The goblins
are going," Kirsty said.
The rest of the bees
had chased the goblins
to the edge of the yard.
Still arguing, the goblins
ran across the fields.

As the grumbling voices faded away,
the icy wind stopped. The sun shone
warmly again and the frost melted. The
bees streamed back and flew around
Rachel and Kirsty, buzzing softly.

"Thank you, Queenie!" Sunny's eyes
sparkled as she hugged her friend.

Suddenly, Queenie wobbled and
tipped sideways.

Rachel cupped her hands,
worried that Queenie
would roll off.
"I think she might
be hurt," she said.
Sunny knelt
down and
looked closely
at Queenie.

"Oh, no! She's torn her wing!"
she gasped.

"It must have happened when
she fought the goblin," Rachel said.

"Can you mend Queenie's wing
with magic?" Kirsty asked Sunny.

Sunny shook her head. "Not
on my own. But Amber or Ruby
might be able to help me. We have
to take Queenie to the pot at the
end of the rainbow right away!"

FAIRY REPAIRS

Rachel and Kirsty hurried across the fields
and into the woods. Rachel carefully
held Queenie in her cupped hands, while
Sunny flew behind them, her rainbow-
colored wings shimmering in the sun.

"There's the willow tree where the pot
is hidden," Kirsty said.

She went over and parted the branches, which hung right down to the ground. The black pot lay on its side in the grass. A large, green frog hopped out from behind it.

"Bertram!" Sunny flew down and hugged him. "I'm so glad you're here!"

Bertram bowed his head. "It's a pleasure, Miss Sunny," he said. "Miss Ruby and Miss Amber will be delighted to see you."

Suddenly, a shower of red and orange fairy dust shot up out of the pot, followed by Ruby and Amber.

"Sunny!" Ruby shouted. "It really *is* you!"

"It's so good to have you back," Amber called happily.

Kirsty and Rachel smiled as the fairies hugged and kissed one another.

The air around them fizzed with red flowers, orange bubbles, and tiny, yellow butterflies.

Ruby flew onto Kirsty's shoulder. "Thank you, Rachel and Kirsty," she said. "Now three of us are safe." Then she spotted Queenie sitting on Rachel's hand. "Who is this?" she asked.

"This is my friend, Queenie," Sunny explained. "She helped me get my wand back after the goblins stole it."

"Goblins?" Ruby shuddered. "You were very brave to fight them, Queenie." She flew down and stroked Queenie's head.

"One of the goblins used my wand to hurt Queenie's wing. Can you help her?" Sunny asked her sisters.

Amber thought hard. "I could mend Queenie's wing if I had a fairy needle and thread," she said. Then she looked sad. "But I don't have any here in the pot."

Then Rachel remembered something.

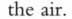

"Kirsty! What about the magic bags that the Fairy Queen gave us?"

"Oh, yes," Kirsty said. She reached into her pocket and pulled out her bag. It was glowing with a soft, silver light. When she opened it, a cloud of glitter shot up into the air.

Kirsty slipped her hand into the bag.

"There's something here." She drew out a tiny, shining needle, threaded with fine spider silk. She held it out to Amber.

"Perfect!" Amber said. She flew onto Rachel's hand and sat next to Queenie.

Sunny stroked Queenie's black-and-yellow head. "Don't worry," she said. "It's fairy magic, so it won't hurt."

Kirsty watched as Amber carefully wove the needle in and out of the torn wing. The row of stitches glowed like tiny silver dots.

"Look, they're starting to fade," Rachel said.

"Yes," said Amber. "When you can't see them anymore, the wing will be healed."

Queenie buzzed softly. She lifted her head and flapped her wings. Then she zoomed into the air. Her wing was as good as new! She swooped down and landed next to Amber. Bowing her head, she rubbed her feelers against the fairy's hand.

"You have been such a good friend to Sunny, you have to stay with us," said Amber, hugging the bee.

"Yes!" Ruby agreed. "Please come and stay with us, just until we go back to Fairyland."

Queenie flew over to Sunny and buzzed in her ear.

"She says she would love to," said Sunny. "There is a hiveless queen in Mrs. Merry's garden who would be happy to take care of her bees. Come on, Queenie. Let's look at our new home."

"Let's take a look too," Kirsty said. Rachel crouched down beside her in the grass. They watched the fairy sisters and the queen bee fly into the pot.

Sunny beamed when she saw all the tiny furniture. She sat down on a soft, mossy cushion. "This is just like our home in Fairyland," she said. Then her face fell.

"But what about our sisters? They are still trapped somewhere on the island!"

"Don't worry," Kirsty said. "We'll find them soon."

"Yes, we will," Rachel agreed, jumping up. She looked at her watch. "It's almost lunchtime. We have to go. But, we'll see you again very soon."

The fairies looked up and waved.

"Good-bye! Good-bye!" Queenie waved a tiny leg and buzzed.

Bertram, the frog footman, followed them out from under the willow tree. "Ruby, Amber, and Sunny will be safe here with me," he said. "But you have to be careful when you go looking for the others. Watch out for goblins!"

"We will," Rachel promised.

Kirsty looked back at the pot at the end of the rainbow. "Nothing will stop us from finding the other Rainbow Fairies!" she said.

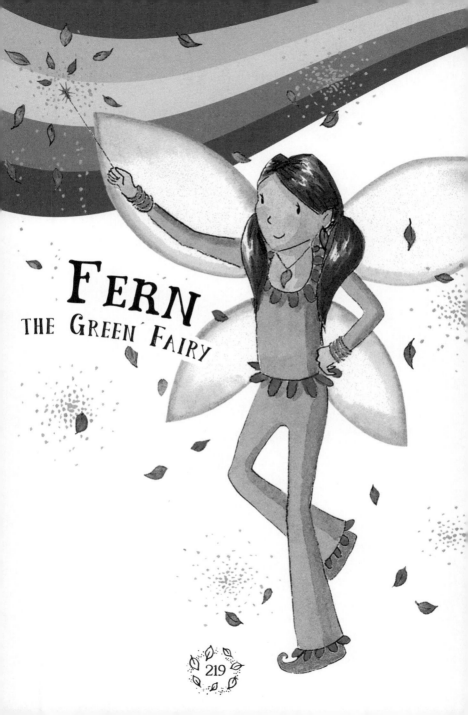

FERN
THE GREEN FAIRY

Cold winds blow and thick ice form,
I conjure up this fairy storm.
To seven corners of the human world
the Rainbow Fairies will be hurled!

I curse every part of Fairyland,
with a frosty wave of my icy hand.
For now and always, from this day,
Fairyland will be cold and gray!

Ruby, Amber, and Sunny are out of danger.

Will Rachel and Kirsty free

FERN the GREEN FAIRY?

Table of Contents

THE SECRET GARDEN

"Oh!" Rachel Walker gasped in delight, as she gazed around her. "What a perfect place for a picnic!"

"It's a secret garden," Kirsty Tate said, her eyes shining.

They were standing in a large garden. It looked as if nobody else had been there for a long, long time.

Pink and white roses grew all around the tree trunks, filling the air with their sweet smell. White marble statues stood here and there, half hidden by green ivy. And right in the middle of the garden was a crumbling stone tower.

"There was a castle here once called Moonspinner Castle," Mr. Walker said, walking up behind them. He was reading from his guidebook. "But now all that's left is the tower."

Rachel and Kirsty stared up at the ruined tower. The yellow stones glowed warmly in the sunshine. They were spotted with soft, green moss. Near the top of the tower was a small, square window.

"It's just like Rapunzel's tower," Kirsty said. "I wonder if we can get up to the top somehow?"

"Let's go see!" Rachel said eagerly. "I want to explore the whole garden. Can we, Mom?"

"Go ahead." Mrs. Walker smiled. "Your dad and I will get the food ready." She opened the picnic basket. "But don't be too long, girls."

Rachel and Kirsty rushed over to the door in the side of the tower. Kirsty tugged at the heavy iron handle. But the door was locked.

Rachel felt disappointed. "Oh, that's too bad," she said.

Kirsty sighed. "Yes, I was hoping Fern the Green Fairy might be here."

Rachel and Kirsty had a secret. During their vacation on Rainspell Island, they were helping to find the seven Rainbow Fairies. The fairies had been sent out of Fairyland by evil Jack Frost, and Fairyland had lost all its color without them. Fairyland would only be bright and beautiful when all seven fairies returned home again.

"Fern," Rachel called in a low voice. "Are you here?"

Here . . . Here . . . Here . . . Her words echoed off the stones. Rachel and Kirsty held their breath and waited. But they couldn't hear anything except leaves rustling in the breeze.

"It *feels* like there's magic close by." Then she gasped and pointed. "Rachel, look at the ivy!"

Rachel stared. Glossy green leaves grew thickly on the wall, but in one place the stones were bare, in the shape of a perfect circle.

Rachel's heart began to beat faster. "It looks just like a fairy ring!" she said. She had heard that when plants grew in a circle, it was the work of fairy magic. She ran around the tower to take a closer look and almost tripped over one of her shoelaces.

"Careful!" Kirsty said, grabbing Rachel's arm.

Rachel sat down on a mossy stone to retie her shoe. "There's green *everywhere*," she said, looking around at the thick grass and the leafy trees. "Fern *must* be here."

"We'd better find her quickly then," Kirsty said with a shiver. "Or else Jack Frost's goblins will find her first!"

Jack Frost had sent his goblin servants to Rainspell Island. He wanted them to stop the fairies from getting home to Fairyland. The goblins were so mean that they made everything around them turn cold and icy.

"Where should we start looking?" Rachel asked, standing up again.

Kirsty looked at her friend and laughed. "You've got green stuff all over you!" she said.

Rachel twisted around to look. The back of her jean skirt was green and dusty. "It must be the moss," she grumbled, brushing it off.

Dust flew up into the air. It sparkled and glittered in the morning sun. As it fell to the ground, tiny, green leaves appeared and the smell of freshly cut grass filled the air.

Rachel and Kirsty turned to each other. "It's fairy dust!" they cried together.

WHERE IS FERN?

"Fern *is* here!" said Kirsty.

"Thank goodness I sat down on that fairy dust!" Rachel said.

They walked all around the tower, looking under bushes and inside sweet-smelling flowers. As they walked, they softly called Fern's name. But the Green Fairy was nowhere to be found.

"You don't think the goblins have already caught her, do you?" Rachel said. She was worried.

"I hope not," replied Kirsty. "I'm sure Fern *was* here, but now it seems like she's somewhere else."

"Yes, but where?" Rachel looked around the garden helplessly.

"Maybe there's magic around to help us," Kirsty said.

She looked down at the tiny leaves. Some of them fluttered across the garden. "I know, let's follow the fairy dust."

The bright green leaves floated over to a narrow path. The path led into a beautiful orchard. Rachel could see apples, pears, and plums growing on the trees.

"It's a magic trail!" Kirsty breathed.

"Quick, let's keep following the fairy dust," Rachel said.

Rachel and Kirsty set off down the path, which twisted and turned through the fruit trees.

Suddenly, the path led them into a large clearing. Kirsty's eyes opened wide when she saw what was in front of them. "It's a maze!" she cried.

The thick, green hedges loomed above them, their leaves rustling softly in the breeze.

Rachel nudged Kirsty. "Look," she pointed. "The fairy trail leads right into the maze!"

"We'll have to take that path," Kirsty said bravely.

The two girls followed the floating fairy leaves through the narrow maze entrance. Kirsty felt a little bit scared as the fairy dust led them one way, then another. What if the trail ran out and they got lost in the maze?

"Maybe there will be another clue in the middle of the maze," Rachel said hopefully.

"Or maybe Fern will be there!" Kirsty added.

They turned one more corner and, suddenly, the hedges parted to reveal the middle of the maze. An oak tree stood in the very center. The fairy dust led right to the bottom of the tree, then stopped.

"Fern must be here!" Rachel said excitedly.

Kirsty frowned. "Yes, but *where*?" she asked, looking around.

Tap! Tap! Tap!

The two girls jumped.

"What was that?" Rachel gasped.

There it was again. *Tap! Tap! Tap!*

Kirsty's eyes opened wide. "It's coming from over there." She pointed to the oak tree.

"I hope it isn't a trap set by the goblins," Rachel whispered.

Tap! Tap! Tap!

The noise was louder now. Slowly, Rachel and Kirsty walked around the tree. At first, they didn't see anything unusual.

Then Rachel pointed at the tree trunk. "What's a *window* doing in a *tree*?" she asked.

There was a small, hollow knot halfway up the trunk—and it was covered by a glass window!

Kirsty put out her hand and touched the window. It was very cold and wet. "It's not glass," she whispered. "It's *ice*!"

Both girls looked more closely. Suddenly, something moved behind the icy window. Kirsty could just barely see a tiny girl dressed in glittering green.

"Rachel, we've found her!" she said happily. "It's Fern, the Green Fairy!"

LOST IN THE MAZE

Fern waved to the girls through the sheet of ice. Her mouth opened and closed, but Rachel and Kirsty couldn't hear a word she was saying. The ice was too thick.

Rachel looked worried. "Fern must be freezing in there," she said. "We have to get her out."

"We could smash the ice with
a stick," said Kirsty. Then she
frowned. "But Fern might get hurt."

Rachel thought hard. "We could
melt the ice," she said.

"How?" Kirsty asked.

"Like this," Rachel replied.
She reached up
and pressed her hand
firmly against the
window of ice.
Kirsty did the
same. The ice
felt freezing
cold, but they
kept on pressing
against it with
their warm hands.

Soon, a few drops of water began to trickle down the window.

"It's melting!" Rachel said. "I think we can make a hole in it now." She gently poked the middle of the window with her finger, and the ice began to crack.

"Don't worry, Fern," said Kirsty. "You'll be out of there very soon!"

There was a sudden crack as the ice split open. A flash of sparkling fairy dust shot out, leaving behind the smell of cut grass. And then Fern the Green Fairy

pushed her way out of the the tree trunk, her wings fluttering limply. She wore a bright green top and stretchy pants, with pretty leaf shapes around her waist and neck. She had small, acorn-colored boots on her tiny feet, earrings, and a pendant that looked like a little green leaf. Her long, brown hair was tied in pigtails, and her thin, emerald wand was tipped with gold.

"Oh, I'm s-s-so c-c-cold!" the fairy gasped, shivering all over. She floated down to rest on Kirsty's shoulder.

"Let me warm you up a bit," said Rachel. She scooped the fairy up and held her in her cupped hands. Then she blew gently on her.

The warmth of Rachel's breath seemed to do the trick. Fern stopped shivering, and her wings straightened out. "Thank you," she said. "I feel much better now."

"I'm Rachel and this is Kirsty," Rachel explained. "We're here to take you to the pot at the end of the rainbow."

"Ruby, Amber, and Sunny are waiting for you," Kirsty added.

Fern's green eyes lit up. "They're safe?" she exclaimed. "That's wonderful!" She flew off Rachel's hand in a burst of green fairy dust and twirled happily in the air. "But what about my other sisters?"

"Don't worry, we're going to find them, too," Kirsty told her. "But how did you get stuck behind that ice window?"

"When I landed on Rainspell Island, I got tangled up in the ivy on the tower," Fern explained. "I managed to untangle myself, but then Jack Frost's goblins started chasing me. So I flew into the maze and hid in the oak tree. It was raining, and when the goblins passed by, their evil magic turned the rainwater to ice. I was trapped."

Suddenly, Rachel shivered. "It's getting colder," she said. She glanced up at the sky. The sun had disappeared behind a cloud, and there was a chill in the air.

"The goblins might be close by!" Kirsty gasped, looking scared.

Fern nodded. "Yes, we should get out of this garden right away," she said calmly. "You know the way, don't you?"

Rachel and Kirsty looked at each other.

"I'm not sure," Kirsty said with a frown. "Do *you* know, Rachel?"

Rachel shook her head. "No," she replied. "But we can follow the fairy trail back to the beginning of the maze."

Kirsty looked around. "Where *is* the fairy trail?" she asked.

An icy breeze was blowing all around them now. The green fairy leaves were drifting away and disappearing.

"Oh no!" Kirsty cried. "What are we going to do now?"

Suddenly, they heard the sound of heavy footsteps coming through the maze toward them.

"I know that fairy is in here *somewhere*," grumbled a loud, gruff voice.

Fern, Rachel, and Kirsty looked at one another with wide eyes.

"Goblins!" whispered Rachel.

FAIRY FIREWORKS

Rachel, Kirsty, and Fern listened in horror as the goblins came closer. As usual, they were arguing with each other.

"Come on!" snorted one goblin. "We can't let her get away again."

"Stop bossing me around," grumbled the other one. "I'm going as fast as I can. OW!"

Just then, there was a loud *THUD!* It sounded like someone had fallen over.

"If your feet weren't so big, you wouldn't trip over them," jeered the first goblin.

"They're big enough to give you a good kick!" the other goblin snapped.

"Let's hide in the tree," Fern whispered to Rachel and Kirsty. "I'll make you fairy-sized, so we can all fit under a leaf."

Quickly, she shot up into the air and sprinkled the girls with fairy dust. Rachel and Kirsty gasped as they felt themselves shrinking, down and down. It was so exciting!

Fern took the girls' hands. "Let's go," she said, and the three of them fluttered up into the air and landed on a branch.

Fat brown acorns grew on the tree, as big as beach balls. Even the thinnest twigs looked like tree trunks to the tiny girls! Fern heaved up the edge of a leaf, which was as big as a tablecloth, and all three of them crept underneath.

A moment later, the goblins rushed into the clearing.

"Where can that fairy be?" grumbled one of them. "I know she came this way!"

They began to search around the bottom of the tree.

"How are we going to get back to the pot?" Rachel whispered to Fern. "Kirsty and I aren't very good at flying. The goblins will catch us if we try!"

Fern laughed. "Don't worry! I think I know someone who can help us!" She pointed behind them.

Rachel and Kirsty turned to look.

A gray, furry face was peeking shyly around the tree trunk. It was a squirrel.

"Hello," Fern called softly.

The squirrel jumped and hid behind the trunk. Then he peeked out again, his dark eyes curious.

"Maybe he'd like an acorn?" Kirsty suggested.

There was a big, shiny acorn growing right next to her. She wrapped her arms around it, but she couldn't pull it off the twig. It was too big! Rachel and Fern came to help. All three of them tugged at the acorn until it came off the branch with a crack.

Fern held the acorn out to the squirrel. "Mmm, a yummy nut!" she said.

The squirrel ran lightly along the branch, his long, furry tail waving. He took the acorn and held it in his front paws.

"What's your name?" asked Fern kindly.

"I'm Fluffy," squeaked the squirrel, between nibbles.

"I'm Fern," said the fairy. "And these are my friends, Rachel and Kirsty. We need to get away from the goblins. Will you help us?"

Fluffy shivered. "I don't like goblins," he squeaked.

"We won't let them hurt you," Fern promised, stroking his head. "Can you give us a ride on your back? You can jump from hedge to hedge much better than we can! We have to get out of the maze."

"Yes, I'll help you," Fluffy agreed, finishing the last piece of his acorn.

Rachel, Kirsty, and Fern climbed onto the squirrel's back. Kirsty thought it was like sinking into a big, soft blanket.

"This is great," said Fern, snuggling down into the squirrel's fur. "Let's go, Fluffy!"

The squirrel turned and ran along the
branch. Rachel, Kirsty, and Fern clung
tightly to Fluffy's thick fur as he jumped
out of the tree, right over the goblins'
heads! He landed on the closest hedge.
The goblins were so busy arguing, they
didn't even notice.

Fern leaned forward to whisper in the squirrel's ear. "Well done, Fluffy. Now, the next one!"

Rachel gulped when she saw how far away the next hedge was. "Maybe Fluffy needs some fairy magic to help him," she said.

"No, he doesn't," Fern replied, her green eyes twinkling. "He'll be fine!"

Fluffy leaped into midair. He sailed across the gap and landed safely on top of the next hedge. Rachel and Kirsty grinned at each other. This was so exciting! It was a bit bumpy, but Fluffy's fur was like a soft cushion. The squirrel was moving so fast, it wasn't long before they had left the goblins far behind.

"We made it!" Fern said at last, as Fluffy reached the edge of the maze. "Now, which way do we go, girls?"

Rachel and Kirsty looked at each other in dismay. "This isn't the way we came *in*," Rachel said. "I don't know the way back to the pot from here. Do you, Kirsty?"

Kirsty shook her head.

Fern looked worried. "But I have to get to the pot!" she said. "That's where my sisters are!"

"Oh!" Kirsty had an idea. "Rachel, what about looking in our magic bags for help?"

"Good idea," Rachel agreed.

Titania, the Fairy Queen, had given Rachel and Kirsty two special magic bags, for whenever they needed help rescuing the fairies. The girls took the bags with them everywhere, just in case.

Kirsty opened her backpack and looked inside. One of the magic bags was glowing with a silvery light. "I wonder what's inside?" she said, reaching in.

She pulled out a thin, green stick covered with sparkling gold stars.

"It looks like a *firework*," Rachel said. "That's not very helpful, is it?"

"It's a fairy firework!" said Fern excitedly. "I can use it to write a message in the sky, and my sisters will see it from the pot. Then they'll know we need help."

"But what about the goblins?" Rachel asked. "Won't they see it, too, and know where we are?"

Fern looked serious. "We have to take the risk," she said. Fern held the firework in one hand, her wings fluttering. She lit the top with her wand and quickly flew up into the sky.

Rachel and Kirsty held their breath. Fern and the sparkler shot upward, trailing bright green sparks behind them. Fern flew

higher and higher into the sky, and
used the sparkler to write a message in a
shower of emerald stars. The stars spelled
out the words:

They twinkled brightly in the darkening
sky before fading away.

"We won't have to wait long," Fern
said, landing beside Rachel and Kirsty on
the ground. "Help will come very soon."

Rachel and Kirsty wondered what was going to happen. How could the fairies come to their rescue? They weren't supposed to leave the pot at the end of the rainbow, in case the goblins found them. Suddenly, the leaves behind Rachel, Kirsty, and Fern rustled.

"Did you see that fairy firework?" shouted a loud goblin voice. "It came from over there. Quick, before that fairy gets away again!"

HEDGEHOG HELP

Rachel and Kirsty looked at each other
in alarm. Fluffy seemed scared, too. The
goblins were on their trail again!

"They're coming toward us,"
Rachel whispered as the goblin voices
got louder.

"Don't worry," Fern said, smiling. She
didn't seem nervous. "My sisters will
send help quickly."

Just then, Rachel spotted a line of golden sparkles twinkling toward them through the fruit trees. "What's that?" she whispered.

"Is it goblin magic?" Kirsty asked, suspicious.

Fern shook her head. "They're fireflies! My sisters must have sent them to show us the way back to the pot."

Suddenly, there was another shout from inside the maze. "Look, what are those lights over there?"

272

"The goblins have spotted the fireflies!"
Rachel gasped.

"Quickly, Fluffy!" Fern said as they all
climbed onto the squirrel's back again.
"Follow the fireflies!"

The golden specks were dancing away
through the trees. Fluffy scampered after
them just as the goblins dashed out of
the maze.

"There's the fairy!" one of them shouted,
pointing at Fern. "Stop that squirrel!"

"Come back!" the other roared as Fluffy
ran off.

Rachel, Kirsty, and Fern clung
to Fluffy's fur as the
squirrel zigzagged
back and forth to
get away from
the goblins. Fluffy
scrambled up the
trunk of the nearest
tree. He was just
about to jump across
to the next tree, when
someone called to them from below.

"Hello!"

"Who's that?" Rachel asked.
She, Kirsty, and Fern peered
down at the ground.

A hedgehog was standing at
the foot of the apple tree.

"Hello!" he hollered again.

"The animals in the garden have heard that you're in trouble. We'd like to help."

"Oh, thank you," Fern called. Then she gasped as the two goblins appeared among the trees.

"Where'd that squirrel go?" one of them yelled.

Quickly, Fluffy leaped across to the next apple tree. The goblins roared with anger and dashed forward. At that moment, the hedgehog curled himself into a ball and rolled right into their path. Rachel thought he looked like a big, prickly soccer ball.

"OW!" both goblins howled. "My toes!"

Rachel and Kirsty couldn't help laughing as the goblins jumped around holding their feet. "Hooray for Hedgehog!" the girls shouted.

As Fluffy jumped from one fruit tree to the next, the firefly lights behind them began to go out.

"Hey! Who turned off the lights?"

wailed one of the goblins, still rubbing his foot. "Which way are we supposed to go?"

"How do I know?" snapped the other goblin. Their voices were getting fainter now as Fluffy hurried on.

"Thank you, fireflies!" called Fern, waving at the last few specks of light. "We need to find a way to the orchard wall from here. We can't be far from the pot now."

"If I were human-sized, I could probably figure out which way to go," Kirsty said. "But everything looks so big and unfamiliar!"

"But if we go back to our normal sizes, the goblins will surely spot us!" said Rachel. "I can help you," a small voice whispered.

A fawn was standing at the bottom of the tree. Her golden brown coat was short and silky, and she stared up at them with big, brown eyes. "You mean you can show us the way?" Kirsty said.

"Yes, I can," the deer nodded, twitching her little tail.

"I can show you a shortcut."

She trotted off through the trees on her long legs. Fluffy followed her, leaping from branch to branch above the little deer's head.

Rachel was so excited she could hardly breathe. She was riding on a squirrel's back, being shown the way to the pot at the end of the rainbow by a fawn!

A few moments later, they reached the brick wall which ran around the outside of the orchard. Fluffy leaped up to the top of the wall, and Rachel and Kirsty looked eagerly ahead of them. On the other side of the wall was a meadow, and beyond that a patch of woods.

"Look!" Rachel shouted. "That's where the pot is!"

FLYING HIGH

"Thank you!" Kirsty and Rachel called to the baby deer. She blinked her long eyelashes at them and trotted away.

A blackbird with shiny, dark feathers was sitting on the wall nearby. He hopped over to them. "I'm here to take you to the pot at the end of the rainbow," he chirped.

"All aboard!"

Fluffy looked sad as Fern, Rachel, and Kirsty slid off his back and climbed onto the blackbird. It was a tight squeeze, and the feathers felt smooth and silky after Fluffy's thick fur.

"Good-bye, Fluffy!" called Rachel. She blew him a kiss. "And thank you!" She felt sad to leave their new friend behind. Then the blackbird soared into the air.

"Look for the big weeping willow tree," Rachel told the blackbird as he swooped over the meadow.

"I can't wait to see my sisters again," said Fern, sounding very excited.

The blackbird flew over the woods and landed in the clearing near the willow tree. Rachel, Kirsty, and Fern jumped down onto the grass, calling good-bye to the blackbird.

"Who's there?" croaked a stern voice.
A plump, green frog hopped out from
under the hanging branches of the tree.

"Bertram, it's me!"
Fern called. Quickly,
the fairy waved her
wand, and Rachel
and Kirsty shot up
to their normal
size again.

"Miss Fern!"
Bertram said joyfully. "You're back!"

"We followed the fireflies," Fern said,
giving the frog a hug. "Thank you for
sending them."

"We saw the firework in the sky,"
Bertram explained, "so we knew you
were in trouble. But you'll be safe here,"
he went on. "The pot is hidden under

the tree. The goblins have no idea that it's here!"

Rachel and Kirsty hurried over and pulled aside the long branches. The pot at the end of the rainbow lay there on its side.

Suddenly, a fountain of red, orange, and yellow fairy dust whooshed out of the pot. Ruby, Amber, and Sunny flew out, looking very excited. A big queen bee buzzed out behind them.

"Fern!" Ruby called. "You're safe!
It's so good to see you!"

Rachel and Kirsty beamed as they
watched the fairies hug one another.
The air around them fizzed and popped
with red flowers, orange bubbles,
yellow butterflies, and green leaves.

"We really missed you," said Sunny. The bee nudged her with a tiny feeler. "Oh, sorry, Queenie," said Sunny. "This is my sister, Fern."

Queenie buzzed, "Hello!"

"How did you get back so quickly?" asked Amber. "We sent the fireflies only a little while ago."

"Our forest friends helped us," Fern said. She waved as the blackbird flew off. "Especially Fluffy the squirrel." She sighed. "It was sad to leave him behind."

Ruby laughed. "Who's that then?" she asked, pointing at a tree on the other side of the clearing.

Rachel and Kirsty looked, too. Fluffy was peeking at them from behind the tree trunk, looking very shy.

"Fluffy!" Fern flew over and hugged him. "What are you doing here?"

"I was worried about you," Fluffy explained shyly. "I wanted to make sure you got back to the pot safely."

"Would you like to stay with us too?" asked Amber. "You could live in the willow tree, couldn't you?"

"Yes, *please*," squeaked Fluffy. "I'm very lonely. I live in that oak tree inside the maze all by myself!"

Ruby turned to Rachel and Kirsty. "Thank you again," she said. "I don't know what we'd do without you!"

Fern fluttered lightly onto Rachel's shoulder. One of her wings brushed softly against Rachel's cheek, like a butterfly. "We'll see you again soon, won't we?"

"Yes, of course," Rachel promised.

"Only three more Rainbow Fairies left to find!" Kirsty added. She took Rachel's hand and they waved to the fairies, then ran out of the clearing. "We'd better get back to your mom and dad, Rachel. They'll be wondering where we are."

"Good idea," Rachel laughed. "If we don't hurry back, my dad will eat the whole picnic by himself!"

Now it's time for Kirsty and
Rachel to help . . .

SKY THE BLUE FAIRY.

Read on for a sneak peek . . .

SKY
THE BLUE FAIRY

A Magic Messenger

"The water's really warm!" Rachel Walker said, laughing. She was sitting on a rock, dipping her toes in one of Rainspell Island's deep, blue tide pools. Her friend Kirsty Tate was looking for shells on the rocks nearby.

"Be careful not to slip, Kirsty!" called Mrs. Tate. She was sitting farther down the beach with Rachel's mom.

"OK, Mom!" Kirsty yelled back. She looked down at her bare feet, and a patch of green seaweed began to move. There was something blue and shiny tangled up in the seaweed. "Rachel! Come over here," she shouted.

Rachel hopped across the rocks. "What is it?" she asked.

Kirsty pointed to the seaweed. "There's something blue under there," she said. "I wonder if it could be . . ."

"Sky the Blue Fairy?" Rachel said eagerly.

A few days before, Rachel and Kirsty had discovered a magical secret. The wicked Jack Frost had banished the seven Rainbow Fairies from Fairyland with a magic spell. Now the fairies were hidden all over Rainspell Island. Until they were all found there would be no color in Fairyland. Rachel and Kirsty had promised the Fairy King and Queen that they would help find the fairies.

The seaweed twitched.

Rachel felt her heart beat faster. "Maybe the fairy is all tangled up," she whispered. "Like Fern when she landed on the ivy in the tower."

Fern was the Green Rainbow Fairy.

297

Rachel and Kirsty had already found Fern and her sisters Ruby, Amber, and Sunny.

Suddenly, a crab crawled out from under the seaweed. The crab was bright blue and very shiny. Tiny rainbows sparkled across its shell.

It didn't look like any of the other crabs on the beach.

Red, orange, yellow, green, blue, indigo, and violet.

Kirsty and Rachel smiled at each other.

This must be more of Rainspell Island's special magic!

"Oh, no! Fairy in trouble!" the crab muttered in a tiny voice. It sounded scratchy, like two pebbles rubbing together.

"Did you hear that?" Rachel gasped.

The crab stopped and peered up at
the girls with his little stalk eyes. Then
he stood up on his back legs.

"What's he doing?" Kirsty asked in surprise.

The crab pointed
a claw toward some
rocks farther along the
beach, under the cliffs.
He rushed forward a
few steps, then came
back and looked up
at Rachel and Kirsty

again. "Over there," he said.

"I think he wants us to follow him,"
Rachel said.

"Yes! Yes!" said the little crab, clicking
his claws. He set off sideways across a
large, flat rock.

Kirsty turned to Rachel. "Maybe he knows where Sky is!"

"I hope so," Rachel replied, her eyes shining.

The crab moved off the rocks and headed across a stretch of sand. Rachel and Kirsty followed him. It was a hot, sunny day. Seagulls flew overhead on strong, white wings.

"Rachel, Kirsty, it's almost lunchtime!" called Mrs. Walker. "We're going back to Dolphin Cottage."

Kirsty looked at Rachel in dismay. "But we have to stay here and look for the Blue Fairy!" she whispered.

The little crab jumped up and down, kicking up tiny puffs of sand. "Follow me, follow me!" he said. The girls couldn't leave him now!

Rachel thought quickly. "Mom?" she called back. "Could we have a picnic here instead, please?"

Mrs. Walker smiled. "Why not? It's a beautiful day. And we should make the most of the last three days of our vacation. I'll head back to the cottage with Kirsty's mom and make some sandwiches."

More Titles to Read

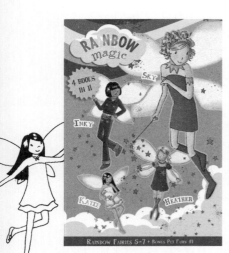

RAINBOW FAIRIES 5–7
+ BONUS PET FAIRY #1

RAINBOW MAGIC SPECIAL EDITION:
HOLLY THE CHRISTMAS FAIRY

☆ ✦ ☆ ☆ ☆ ✦ ☆

BEHIND THE MAGIC

DAISY MEADOWS is a pseudonym for the
four writers of the internationally bestselling *Rainbow Magic* series: Narinder
Dhami, Sue Bentley, Linda Chapman, and
Sue Mongredien. *Rainbow Magic* is the no.1
bestselling series for children ages 5 and up
with over 40 million copies sold worldwide!

GEORGIE RIPPER was born in London and
is a children's book illustrator known for
her work on the *Rainbow Magic* series of
fairy books. She won the Macmillan Prize
for Picture Book Illustration in 2000 with
My Best Friend Bob and *Little Brown Bushrat*,
which she wrote and illustrated.